The Heffalump Grump

For Jude and Jasmine
H.O.
For the Grump in all of us . . .
L.G.

ORCHARD BOOKS
338 Euston Road, London, NW1 3BH
Orchard Books Australia
Hachette Children's Books
17/207 Kent Street, Sydney, NSW 2000

ISBN 1 84362 792 2

First published in Great Britain in 2005
First paperback edition published in 2006

Text © Hiawyn Oram 2005
Illustrations © Lindsey Gardiner 2005

The right of Hiawyn Oram and Lindsey Gardiner to be identified
as the author and illustrator of this work has been asserted by
them in accordance with the Copyright, Designs and Patents Act, 1988.

A CIP catalogue record for this book is available from the British Library.

1 3 5 7 9 10 8 6 4 2

Printed in China

The Heffalump Grump

Hiawyn Oram
Lindsey Gardiner

YAWNNN!

ORCHARD BOOKS

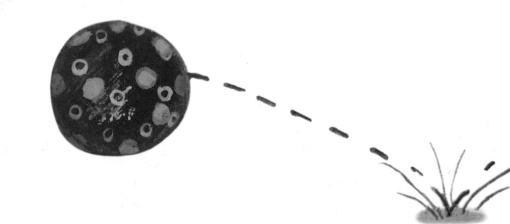

The plump little prince . . .

was in a hump . . .

a terrible hump . . .

a heffalump's GRUMP.

"Oh dear!"
cried his mum.

"Oh dear!"
cried his dad.

"Whatever could ever
be quite this bad?"

"BAAAH!" went the prince.

And the **GRUMP** got worse.

"Bring toys," cried his mum.
"Bring more and more!"

"Bring them all," cried his dad.

"Bring the whole toy store!"

"BAAAH!" went the prince.

And the **GRUMP** got worse.

"Bring cakes," cried his mum.
"And sweet sugared plums.

Ice cream and chocolates
and bright-coloured gums!"

"BAAAH!"
went the prince.

And the **GRUMP** got worse.

"Get pets!" cried his dad.
"And a kangaroo . . .

. . . elephants, tigers,

the London Zoo!"

"BAAAH!"
went the prince.

And the
GRUMP
got worse.

"Try puppets,"
cried his mum,
"and some acrobats!"

"Call clowns," cried his dad,
"and some circus cats!"

"BAAH-NAAH!"
went the prince.

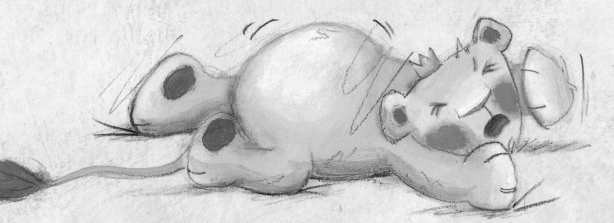

And the **GRUMP** got worse.

"That's it!" cried his mum.
"We've done what we can!

We need to get help.
We need to find Gran!"

"Aha!" said his gran.
"In the case of a **GRUMP**...

as big as a heffalump's
heffa-sized hump . . .

. . . I'll choose him one toy,
this ragged old bear,

with buttons for eyes
and a chewed left ear.

Then I'll sit him down
in my warm safe lap.

The perfect place for a
GRUMPLESS nap.

And I'll sing him a song
of all being right,
as I rock him gently
and hold him tight."

And, as any **GRUMP** will,
if you know how to treat it . . .

...the **GRUMP** disappeared,
it vanished, it beat it.

"Thanks, Gran," said the prince,
as he went off to bed.

"It only began . . .

. . . 'cause I couldn't find Ted!"

Goodnight!